ARTY AND THE HUNT
FOR PHANTOM

ARTY AND THE HUNT FOR PHANTOM

By
Mark L. Redmond

Illustrated by
Laura Ury

SWORD of the LORD PUBLISHERS

P. O. Box 1099, Murfreesboro, TN 37133

Printed and Bound in the United States of America

CHAPTER ONE

Just like any other cowboy who tells a story about himself, I reckon I'm sometimes guilty of leaving out some of the parts that I don't want folks to know. This isn't one of those times.

With hundreds of acres of our ranch just begging to be explored and my pony, Prince, whinnying to me, chores were the last things I wanted to be doing on a beautiful summer morning. As I closed the ranch house door behind me on this particular morning, I knew they were the first things that had to be done.

The one good thing about my morning chores was that most of them were helping Grubby, our cook. I can't say I liked the work I had to do, but I did like listening to the stories he told me while we worked. I didn't know how old Grubby was, but he was at least as old as my Grandpa Anderson. He had been in a lot of Indian fights, done some exploring and tried just about every exciting thing at least once.

The ranch hands had eaten and then ridden off in several directions to begin their day's work. I was helping Grubby clean up after them and get out his supplies for supper that night. Since most of the hands would be too far away to ride back for their noon meal, Grubby always had something they could take in their saddlebags to keep them until they came back for supper.

"Were all Indians bad, Grubby?" I asked.

He poured two cups of coffee from the big metal pot on the stove, handed one to me and took a biscuit from the plate that was still sitting on the corner of the table. "Sit a spell, Arty, and help yourself to something else to eat if you still have room." He sat in one of the chairs at the table, and I sat down across from him. He chewed on a mouthful of biscuit, swished some coffee around in his mouth and swallowed.

"No more than all white folks is bad," he answered. "They's people just like us, who laugh and cry and love and hate and fight and die. I know—I lived with a tribe for a while—married a squaw, one of the best women I've ever known!"

"What happened to her?" I asked.

After taking another drink, he set his cup on the table and sighed. "Well, while I was out with a hunting party one day, some bounty men come along and killed all our women, children and old folks; so when we came back to camp, we found only the dead."

"Why would someone do a thing like that?" I asked.

"Well, in them days the government was trying to stop some of the wild young bucks who had been doing some raiding. A bounty was offered for scalps. Some men didn't care where they got 'em, and the government didn't ask no questions."

I was fighting back tears as I stammered, "I'm sorry, Grubby. How awful! How could you stand it?"

He stared at the table in front of him and said, almost in a whisper, "Well, son, I couldn't. I went after those men, and I caught up with them. There were five. At their camp one night I hailed them, and they called me in to their fire. I made sure there was only five of 'em; then I leveled my Winchester at 'em and told 'em they was gonna die. One of 'em grabbed for his gun, and then things really got hot. When the smoke cleared, they was all dead, and I was shot to pieces. I was laid up for months, but I got my strength back directly. After that, I was never good for anything but cookin'. That's how I come by the handle 'Grub.'"

I knew I was staring, and before I had taken

time to think, I blurted out, "You were wrong to kill those men, Grubby. God says He'll take care of vengeance."

He drank the rest of his coffee, set his cup on the table and looked at me. "You talk like my wife used to, son. She got religion from some missionary folk that come to her village when she was little. She almost had me thinkin' there was something to all that stuff, but when she was killed, I knew she was wrong. A God like she believed in couldn't be what He said He was and still let things like that happen."

I felt like I did the time Jim Nelson punched me in the stomach back in Ohio. "You mean you don't believe in God—you're not a Christian?" I asked.

Grubby stared into his empty cup and replied, "Pshaw—what good did bein' a *Christian* do my Little Fawn? She's dead, ain't she? And I'm alone. For that matter, what good did bein' a *Christian* do your pa? I hear he was a religious man, but you and your ma is still alone, ain't you? The way I see things, religion may be fine for some folks, but not for me."

We finished our work in silence, but I was praying for a chance to help Grubby and hoping God would take away his bitterness. The more I thought about God's letting Pa die and about what Grubby had said, the more I realized that I needed some help with bitterness too.

As I walked back to the house, I still had that feeling in my stomach.

CHAPTER TWO

"You wanted to see me, Luke?" Ma was sitting at her writing desk when Marshal Bodie walked into the den. I put down my copy of *Great Expectations* and tried to pretend that I was surprised to see him.

I had never seen the marshal act this way before. With hat in hand, he stood first on one foot, then shifted to the other while he looked around the room as if he'd never seen it before.

"No, Miss Elizabeth, I didn't want to see—well, I didn't mean that I didn't want to see you, of course—I'm always happy to see you. What I meant was that I didn't have any particular reason to see you. I was just riding out this way— uh—and I thought I'd stop by."

Ma smiled as only she could smile and said, "Sit down then. Would you like a cup of coffee or some lemonade?"

"Oh—yes, lemonade, please."

"I'll get you some too, Arty; you're always thirsty."

As soon as Ma had left, the marshal looked at me and smiled. "Don't worry, son, I'll ask her; just give me a minute or two."

"But I can't wait—and can't you just *tell* her instead of asking her? You're almost like family, and—"

"Arty, hold your horses!" he said, laughing.

"This isn't a legal matter, so I don't reckon I have any authority over your ma. I need to persuade her, not order her."

We stood as Ma came back into the room, and then we sat, sipping our lemonade and talking about a hundred boring things like cattle, the ranch, the weather and a cougar that had been killing some stock recently. Finally, Marshal Bodie brought the subject around to where I had wanted it to be all along.

"Elizabeth, Arty tells me he's thirteen now; and, well, he does a lot of riding alone. I think it's time for him to start carrying some protection with him."

Ma put down her lemonade as if it had been poisoned and asked in almost a whisper, "You mean he should start carrying a gun?"

"Well, Elizabeth, most boys his age do. Of course, Bill and I would be sure to train him first so that he'd know how to handle a gun before we let him carry one."

"You mean you'd teach him how to kill?" Ma had one or two of those red splotches on her neck, so I knew she was either scared or angry. I guessed she was scared.

"Elizabeth, a gun is just a tool, like the shovel or the hoe of a farmer or the hammer of a black-smith. It's a tool a man needs if he's to get his job done."

"How many wounds did you see last year that

came from a shovel or hoe or hammer compared to the number you saw that came from guns?"

"Now, Elizabeth, you know that's not a fair question. I know you've made a lot of adjustments in changing from life in an Ohio town to life on a Texas ranch—and you've done well too—and I know that the idea is a strange one to you, but, believe me, it's time to train the boy to use a gun. If he were my son and you were my..." He stopped, red-faced, backed up and started again. I thought I saw just a bit of a smile on Ma's face. "If he were my son, I'd do just what I'm asking you to let me do now. Please trust me—and trust Arty."

The splotches were still on Ma's neck, and she looked worried, but she smiled. I walked over to her. She stood, put her arms around me and gave me a hug. I felt older somehow—more like the man of the house—not because I was going to carry a gun, but because Ma trusted me enough to let me carry one.

* * *

Early the next morning Arty the Kid stood in front of the saloon, leaning on the hitching rail. I was dressed completely in black. At each hip, in a black holster with silver studs, hung a .44 six-shooter with a pearl handle. My hat was tipped back on my head, and a long piece of straw hung from the corner of my mouth.

Facing the door to the saloon, I drawled, "Rafe Alman and Jeff Chastain, I know you're in there.

*Come out in the daylight, you sneakin' polecats. I'll
face you one at a time or together."*

*I drew my guns from their holsters, spun them
around on my fingers, and re-holstered them in
one lightning-quick movement.*

*The saloon doors swung open. Rafe Alman
walked into the street, hands in the air and sweat
dripping from his face. "P-please don't kill me,
Kid. I never meant no harm to you or your ma. It
was Jeff. He's the one who—"*

*"Be quiet, you vermin. You're going to pay for
what you've done. Where's your beady-eyed little
partner?"*

"Right behind you, Anderson."

*Without looking around, I knew Jeff Chastain
had already drawn his gun and had it pointed at
me. In one quick movement I whipped out both six-
guns and shot both men's guns from their hands
before they could fire a single shot. Once again, the
six-guns spun in my hands and slipped back into
their holsters.*

*Marshal Bodie came from his office, wiped his
mouth with his sleeve and shook my hand.
"Thanks, Kid. The whole town owes you."*

*"Think nothin' of it, Luke. I was just doin' a
favor for my friends."*

* * *

"Well, how about doing me another favor and
strapping this on yourself."

I jumped at the sound of the marshal's voice. The town and the outlaws were gone. I was standing in Coyote Canyon, where I'd been waiting for Marshal Bodie to meet me for my first shooting lesson. I reckon I'd been too busy shooting at outlaws to hear the marshal ride up. I could feel my cheeks burning with embarrassment now as I tried to think of some way to explain my actions. The marshal's chuckle made me relax, and then I saw what he was holding out to me.

"It's yours, pardner. I ordered it awhile back, and it came in on the stage a couple of weeks ago. It's nothing fancy, but it will be reliable and should last a good while if you take care of it."

"Thanks, Marshal," I said, swallowing a lump in my throat. I looked at the gun with its smooth wooden handle and plain brown holster. It was nothing like the guns I had worn a few minutes earlier, but it was real.

I buckled the belt and tied the holster down with the leather thong fastened to the bottom of it.

"As I said, it's nothing fancy, Arty, but it's lightweight, well-made and accurate. Want to try it?"

"Is it loaded?" I asked.

"Do I bait your hook when we're fishing?" He handed me a box of ammunition and showed me how to load a gun without pointing it at anyone. Then he explained that a cowboy who had some riding to do always left one chamber in the gun's cylinder empty. He kept the empty chamber under

the gun's hammer so that if he got any kind of bump or jar while riding, the gun wouldn't go off accidentally and shoot him in the leg or foot.

After I had loaded my gun, Marshal Bodie set up some empty bean tins on the branches of a greasewood bush about twenty paces away.

"Now, Arty, you point that gun the way you point your finger. Squeeze that trigger gently, and see if you can hit one of those tins."

I turned toward the bush, drew my gun, pointed at one of the tins, pulled the hammer back and squeezed the trigger. Five more times I cocked the gun and fired. Then while I waited for the smoke to clear, I tried to think of the nicest way to tell the marshal that I was too close to the bush. Shooting from this distance was too easy.

When the smoke had disappeared, I couldn't believe my eyes! Not one tin had been knocked off the bush. When I walked closer and looked again, I saw that there wasn't even a scratch on any of the tins. I looked at the marshal standing beside me. He was hatless with his feet spread, his arms crossed, watching me.

"Well, I don't think you hurt 'em, pard; but if they had legs, they sure enough would be running scared." He chuckled, stooped and picked up his hat. He held it toward me with his finger sticking through a hole in the crown. "I'd be running scared too if I had a lick of sense!"

"Marshal, did I do that?" I asked. I was beginning

to feel sick, but then the marshal grinned at me.

"No, son, this is an old hat that someone else put a bullet through a long time ago." He dusted it off and put it back on his head. "I just wore it as a joke on you. But seriously, there are some things to remember about handling a gun. For one thing, you never point your gun at someone unless you're prepared to shoot him. Also, you always treat a gun as if it was loaded, even if you're sure it's empty. Plenty of folks have been killed by guns that people thought were empty but turned out not to be. Now, reload and try again."

My fourteenth shot knocked a tin off the bush. So did my eighteenth. Marshal Bodie had work to do, so he left me to practice. During the next two hours, I hit a few more tins; but when I mounted Prince and headed for home, I knew I wouldn't have to bring any more tins for the next day— unless I brought some bigger ones.

I was up early the next morning and back out at the canyon. I had my gun, several boxes of ammunition, a couple of biscuits and some jerky, a canteen of water and another of coffee, and my Bible. I practiced shooting for awhile and hit three or four cans—not always the ones I aimed for, but a hit is a hit. Then I spent some time reading my Bible and praying. I read from my favorite book, Joshua. I'd always liked the battles and the way God had worked again and again to help Joshua defeat his enemies. I put down my Bible, and with a biscuit in my left hand, I turned toward the tin bush.

"So, you Amalekite dog, you think you can stand against the servant of the God of Israel, do you? Well, have some of this!"

I drew my gun and fired five quick shots, kicking up dust on one side of the bush, clipping off a branch about the size of my finger and then hitting three tins in a row—the three I was aiming at!

For the rest of the summer I practiced for a while almost every day—except Sundays, of course. Sometimes Marshal Bodie or our foreman, Bill, or Chad or one of the other men from the ranch came with me. They teased, instructed and encouraged me when they came; and they entertained me with stories of their first attempts at shooting or tales of adventures they had had when they had been my age.

On a Saturday morning in early September, I was practicing for the last time before school started when Marshal Bodie rode up. He nodded to me and smiled, "Good morning, Arty the Kid. Are you ready to trade in your gun for a slate and some schoolbooks? I hear that Miss Ross is back from visiting her folks in the East, and she's ready to try another year of teaching."

He dropped his hand to his side, looked at me sternly and said, "Give up your gun and your evil ways, Kid; I'm takin' you in to school. Do your time, and maybe you'll be out in eight or ten years."

I narrowed my eyes and dropped my hand to my side, turning to face the marshal. He had dismounted and stood about ten feet from me. "I ain't comin' back with you, Marshal. You know that bein' locked up in school would make me crazy. You either ride away or make your play."

"I'm gonna' have to shoot the top tin off your bush, Kid," said the marshal. "Don't make me do that."

"You're goin' to have to try, Marshal. Make your move."

"You draw first, Kid. I want to give you a chance."

The bush was about twenty-five feet away on my right. One of the tins on it was higher in the branches than the others. I turned toward the bush and drew my gun in one quick movement. I pointed and fired, and the tin flew into the air. But before it hit the ground, I heard the marshal's gun, and the falling tin leaped into the air again— and again and again and again. Four times he hit the tin before it finally rolled to a stop on the ground about fifty feet away. He reloaded his gun, twirled it on his finger and flipped it back into its holster.

As soon as I could close my mouth I stammered, "I-I'll go to school, Marshal." Then we both laughed. "I have two questions, Marshal. First, will I ever be able to shoot like that? And second, why did you only shoot four times instead of five?"

Marshal Bodie rubbed his chin thoughtfully for a minute. "Well, Arty the Kid, the second question is the easier of the two to answer. Pa always taught me that when it was possible, I should save one bullet—just in case. He said that the difference between an empty gun and a gun with one bullet in it could be the difference between life and death. So I always try to keep one bullet in my gun until I can reload—just in case.

"The first question is a harder one to answer, but judging by the way you've taken so quickly to using a gun, I'd say you're what folks call a natural shooter. I think you'll be better than I am someday or at least faster on the draw. There's a whole lot more to staying alive and out of trouble than just being a fast draw and a good shot though, and teaching you all you need to know will take years.

"I was heading toward your house; your ma invited me to dinner. Want to ride with me?"

One invitation to go home for a midday meal was enough for me. I was on Prince's back without using a stirrup and ready to go in no time at all. As dry as the dust was on the way home, my mouth was watering at the thought of Ma's cooking.

CHAPTER THREE

I was glad to get back to school that fall. Oh, I missed the freedom of roaming our ranch, but I was glad to be back with Miss Ross and my schoolmates—especially Esther Travis. She was brown from being in the sun and prettier than ever.

That first Monday morning I was up before the sun rose, working at my chores. By sunup I was eating breakfast with the ranch hands, and when Ma came in for breakfast, I was ready to head for town.

Ma smiled when she saw me. "Why, Mr. Anderson, what a handsome young man you are! But what is this? Are you going away? Do not forsake me in my hour of need!" Ma had her hands clasped like she was praying, and she looked heartbroken except for the twinkle in her eyes.

I hooked my thumbs in my pockets and spoke in my best cowboy drawl; "I have to leave, Miss 'Lizabeth; but I'll be back for you. If I have to crawl through blazing rivers and raging deserts, I'll—" Ma interrupted me by bursting out laughing.

"*Blazing* rivers and *raging* deserts?" she giggled. I laughed too, but I finished my say.

"That's right, ma'am. Always remember that nothing stops an Anderson, and you got the word of Arty the Kid on that."

Ma clasped her hands again after wiping away

a tear from laughter. "But, Kid, you can't leave me now."

"But you can't, I tell you!"

"Why not, my little prairie chicken?" Ma giggled for a minute, but she put on a most serious look again and said, "You can't leave me because I don't have your lunch packed yet!" She threw her arms around me. I hugged her, and we both laughed.

After Ma had put three pieces of chicken, two buttered slices of bread and a big piece of apple pie in my lunch tin, I kissed her goodbye. I took my gun belt from the peg by the door and fastened the belt around my waist. Ma looked a little worried for a minute, but when she realized I was looking back at her, she smiled. "You will be careful with that gun, won't you, Artemus? I mean, you won't let it go off and shoot your foot or anything?"

"Aw, Ma, I'm not a baby anymore. This gun is a tool, and I've worked hard this summer to learn to use it. I can use it too! Bill and Marshal Bodie both say that I have a natural talent for handling a gun, but I have enough respect for it that I won't use it like a toy. Please trust me, Ma."

She smiled again. "I'm sorry, Arty. I do trust you. It's just that you're still so young, and I guess sometimes I don't want you to grow up so fast. Please forgive me."

I let Prince have his head as we started toward

town. The day was clear, and I felt like singing a song. I was just about to let loose with "A Mighty Fortress Is Our God" when some movement in the rocks to my right caught my eye. I was only about a hundred yards away from those rocks, and I had plenty of time to get to school, so I decided to see just what kind of varmint was over there.

It had looked to be something big—too big for a jackrabbit or a prairie dog, and it was the wrong color. I figured it must be a deer or an antelope. I rode closer, my eyes scanning the rocks for more movement. I was about to turn Prince back toward town when I saw the dead calf. It had been killed and partially eaten. Judging from the small amount of meat missing and the puddle of blood on the ground, I concluded it was a fresh kill. I had interrupted somebody's breakfast, but whose?

Well, about that time I remembered something our foreman had told me not long after I got Prince. "A smart cowboy listens to his horse," he had said. "This pony can hear better, smell better and run faster than you can. When he senses trouble, he'll warn you. You just be sure you're smart enough to pay attention to him."

Prince's ears were back, and he began to snort and prance around. I let him go, and he took off for town at a full gallop. I decided to stop by those rocks on the way home from school to investigate when I'd have more time.

I put Prince in the common corral after I'd stripped off his saddle and bridle and made sure there was water in the trough. Then I wandered over to the schoolhouse. I still had half an hour or so before the other students would begin to arrive, and I thought I might find Miss Ross in need of some help. As I walked down the street toward the schoolhouse, I thought about what had happened on this day last year. I had made a fool of myself by lying to impress a pretty girl, who had turned out to be my teacher.

I had gotten off to a bad start with Miss Ross, but over the course of a year, I had earned her trust by being totally honest with her and the other students. I was sure she'd forgotten all about that day because she'd never mentioned it again.

The door to the schoolhouse was open, so I knocked and stepped inside. As my eyes made the adjustment from bright sunlight to a darker class-room, I saw Miss Ross at her desk, reading. The morning sunlight came through the window beside her and made her long, red hair glow like the embers of winter fire when hit by a draft.

She looked up from her book and smiled a smile that made my heart skip a beat. This beautiful lady, though my teacher, was only six or seven years older than I was.

"Good morning, Artemus," she said, putting a marker in her place and closing her book. "Come in and tell me about your summer. Has anything exciting happened that I haven't heard about, or..." She stopped; then I realized that she had seen my six-gun.

"Well, I see that you're armed. Can you use that gun, or is it for decorative purposes?" She winked as she spoke.

"Can you spare a moment to step outside?" I asked, resting my hand on the gun's butt.

We went around behind the schoolhouse. I found a few pieces of dead wood, which I threw as far as I could toward the little creek that ran behind the buildings on that side of the street. I drew my gun and fired three quick shots, hitting a stick two of the three times.

Miss Ross clapped her hands. "Good shooting, Arty! Might I have a try?"

Trying not to smile, I handed her my gun and looked around for a bigger target. I walked over to where the pieces of wood lay, looking for the biggest piece.

"Arty," Miss Ross called, "do you have a pencil?"

I fetched one from my pocket and held it up.

"Would you please stick it in the top of that old stump over to your right—with the point up? Does it have a good point?"

I checked, and it did, though I couldn't imagine why that fact would make any difference. She couldn't be planning to shoot at a target that small. I walked back to where she was standing. I could see the pencil, but I didn't think I could hit it from that far away—and I was sure she couldn't.

She raised that gun with one smooth, easy motion and fired, but the pencil was still there. She smiled and handed my gun back to me. "I think I hear some more students arriving. That's a good gun, Arty; don't forget to reload. Just hang it on a peg in the back of the room." She turned and walked back to the school, and I went to fetch my pencil.

I felt a little sorry for her and wished I could've found a bigger target, but then women aren't supposed to be great shooters—she knew that. I picked up my pencil and was about to shove it back into my pocket when I noticed something that couldn't be true. About an inch of it had been neatly clipped off by Miss Ross's bullet! I looked

back at the schoolhouse. She was just rounding the corner, but she stopped and looked back at me and smiled again. "You can sharpen it with your jackknife, Arty."

I leaned against the front of the schoolhouse for the next ten minutes or so, waiting for Esther to come, sharpening my pencil, letting everybody see that I was wearing a gun and wondering where Miss Ross had learned to shoot.

Finally, the Travis girls came—Mary and Ruth holding hands and Esther walking behind them. I had seen Esther at church every Sunday during the summer, and we had gone riding together five or six times; but each time I saw her, I felt like I must have forgotten how pretty she'd been the last time I'd seen her. I was usually uncomfortable around a pretty girl, but with Esther I was always...well...at ease, I guess.

We had time for a quick hello, and then Miss Ross rang the bell to let us know school was about to begin.

I hung up my gun belt and sat down beside a new boy. He was my size and about my age, but the likeness ended there. I was as brown as most Indians; he was pale and freckled. My eyes and hair were brown; he had blond hair and blue eyes.

"I'm Arty Anderson," I whispered. He grinned and whispered back, "I'm Tom Green."

I don't claim to understand the reasons that make people best friends from their first meeting.

I don't even know if there are any reasons. I only know that from that minute, Tom Green and I were best friends.

CHAPTER FOUR

That first day of school sure did seem to be over in a hurry. I stood outside and talked to Tom for a while after everyone else had gone. Tom, his ma and pa, his younger brother, and his twin sisters had come west from Pennsylvania during the summer. Dr. Green, Tom's pa, planned to set up practice right here in White Rock. I reckon Doc Green must have had a good practice in Pennsylvania because from our conversation I learned that the family seemed to have plenty of money for whatever they needed.

"We ain't really rich though, Arty," Tom explained. "I think my pa has just saved his money for a long time."

I told Tom all about our ranch and Ma, and then we walked over to the livery stable. Tom's mouth dropped open when I introduced him to Prince.

"You mean Prince belongs only to you—he's nobody else's?" he asked. "Do you think he could hold me?" I laughed and promised him a ride on Prince as soon as we could work things out for him to come to the ranch for a visit. He waved goodbye and trotted down the street toward his house, which was just outside the other end of town.

As I stroked Prince's powerful neck, my thoughts turned from the Greens to Jasper Wilson and his folks. Before they got born again and took over the store, I hadn't had much occasion to keep company with them. From that first Sunday dinner though, I started learning things about them, and the more I learned, the better I liked them.

There were just the three of them. Mrs. Wilson told Ma they had always wanted to have more children, but none had come along yet. Mrs. Wilson was a bit on the plump side. Her pretty face most of the time wore a warm, genuine smile, and hearing her laugh always seemed to make me want to laugh too. As I spent more time around the family, I began to notice that whenever Jasper had something to say, his ma had time to listen—just like mine.

Mr. Wilson was about average in height, thin, wiry and quick in his movements. He was quiet, patient, hardworking, soft-spoken and about as friendly as any man I'd ever known. I couldn't imagine anyone being in his right mind and not liking Mr. Wilson.

Now, how two people like them had come to have a son like Jasper is more than I could hope to guess. Both of his parents loved him, and they had made him do right even before they got born again. They were good parents, and Jasper was a good kid, but he was—well, he was just hard to explain.

I recalled one hot summer day. Jasper, his pa and I had just finished unloading three wagonloads of supplies. We were soaked with sweat, and Mr. Wilson had brought out three bottles of soda—"sarsaparilla" he called it. We were all three leaning with our backs against the hitching rail. Jasper's pa took a big swig from his bottle, sloshed the cool liquid around in his mouth, then spat it out on the dusty street.

Jasper and I saw what he had done. I took a swig from my bottle, sloshed it around in my mouth, then spat it out on the dusty street. Jasper was quiet for a minute, then he gulped a huge mouthful of his sarsaparilla, sloshed it around in his mouth, then spat it out—on his father's pant leg! Mr. Wilson's expression never changed. He looked from his pant leg to Jasper, to me and then back to his pant leg. "Son," he said, "fetch me my rifle." Everything was quiet for a minute. Then Mr. Wilson rubbed Jasper's head and laughed out loud. "I reckon I've been neglecting this boy's education," he said, grinning at me. "We got to have him some target practice."

Another time that same summer, Jasper and his pa had been after a mouse they had cornered in the store. When I came in, Jasper had a corn broom in his hand, and his pa was on his hands and knees in front of a stack of canned goods. He whispered to Jasper, "I'll slide this stack of tins back away from the corner until there's room to get at the mouse. Don't get in a hurry. In fact, watch me for a signal. When I nod my head, you clobber it with your broom."

Jasper had a confused look on his face, and I was pretty sure I knew what was about to happen. Mr. Wilson slid the stack of canned goods back slowly and nodded at Jasper, who hit him in the head with the broom. Tins went flying, and Mr. Wilson was sprawled out on the floor. The mouse disappeared. I disappeared too—laughing and wondering if Miss Ross shouldn't teach Mr. Wilson a lesson about pronouns and antecedents!

Mr. Wilson had been a farmer in Pennsylvania, but after two years of drought and a losing battle with some locusts, he had decided to sell his farm and move west, hoping to buy a small ranch or get into some kind of business. But while the family was coming through Kansas, some highwaymen had held them up and robbed them of all their money.

The Wilsons had come as far as White Rock,

Texas on money that Mr. Wilson had earned by doing odd jobs along the way. They had been talking of moving on when they met Ma. She had hired Mr. Wilson to run the store, which she had just bought. Mr. Wilson had been thrilled with his new position, and I know he and Ma had talked about a partnership somewhere down the road.

Mr. Wilson ran the store most of the time. Mrs. Wilson helped when things got busy or when Mr. Wilson had to go after supplies.

While he was away on one of those trips, I stopped by the store to see Jasper. He was standing behind the counter listening to his ma when I walked in.

"Now, Jasper, chances are no one will even come in while I'm gone. I just have to take this money to the bank and then stop in at Widow Smith's place. She's ailing, and I told her I'd stop by to pick up a list of things she needs. You can take them to her later today. I'll be back as soon as—oh, come in, Arty. If you're not in a hurry, I'd be obliged if you'd help Jasper keep an eye on things until I return."

I told Mrs. Wilson I had nothing else planned and would be happy to stay with Jasper. Promising again to be right back, she smiled at us and left. I had my back to Jasper and was still facing the door when I heard Jasper's voice, as deep as he could get it: "Can I help you with something today, friend?" Jasper's pa welcomed customers the same way. Jasper was standing like his pa, thumbs hooked in his suspenders, grinning at me.

I grinned back. "How about selling me a couple of those peppermint sticks?" I asked. "I'll share with you."

Just then the door opened and a stranger walked in. He was over six feet tall, covered with dust and looked to be angry at the world. He glanced at us and then started walking up and down, picking up items from the shelves. He put an armload of supplies on the counter and then went back and picked up a few more things. "Who runs this place?" he growled.

Jasper squinted at the man and said in his store voice, "I do. Can I help you with something today, friend?"

The stranger looked a bit surprised but said, "How much do I owe you?"

Jasper took the pencil from behind his ear and began to add on a pad of paper, mumbling like his father as he wrote. I thought he was adding too quickly, then I heard part of what he was mumbling. He picked up a tin of peaches and a plug of tobacco and placed them on the other side of his pad, mumbling to himself, "One if by land, two if by sea."

"Hurry up, kid. I ain't got all day," the stranger growled, slapping his hand on the counter. I pulled the price list from under the counter and helped Jasper figure out the bill.

"Two dollars and two bits," said Jasper.

"That seems a little high to me," the stranger remarked.

"Two dollars and two bits," Jasper said, lowering his voice to the deepest pitch he could.

The stranger glared at him but dug the money out of his vest pocket and slapped it on the counter. Jasper crammed the purchases into a feed sack, and the man picked up his sack and stomped out, muttering to himself.

A few minutes later Mrs. Wilson returned, and Jasper assured her that all had gone well during her absence. She looked at me, and I shrugged my shoulders and handed Jasper his peppermint stick. He thanked me and grinned.

I looked at his skinny neck and his turtle head with its hacked-up haircut and grinned back because I was happy to have Jasper for a friend.

I wasn't in any particular hurry, so I took my time getting Prince saddled and bridled. I found myself smiling as I thought about Miss Ross and how this pretty lady from Connecticut had come to be teaching school in Texas. Her pa had been a circuit-riding preacher for a spell before he met her ma. After her parents got married, the reverend decided to settle in one area and quit riding the circuit. He started his own church, which he helped to populate by having nine children. Miss Ross was the third of those children.

The oldest of the Ross children was Sam, who had married and decided to become a banker. He had been very hardworking and successful—so successful that when the bank's owners opened a new bank in Amarillo, Texas, they had asked Sam to be its manager.

Miss Ross had finished her schooling by then and wanted to teach, so when Sam announced that he was headed west, Miss Ross got her parents' permission to go with him and his family. They had arrived in Amarillo just as the school year ended. Someone from White Rock had heard of Miss Ross's arrival. She had been offered the schoolteacher's job and had accepted it.

Now, Miss Ross was not just a lady with a pretty smile and a pleasant personality. Ma said that she was one of those women who was pretty from the inside out. She was intelligent, sweet, thoughtful, kind and generous. She could cook and sew and had a pretty singing voice too. She wasn't married, not because she hadn't been asked, but because she hadn't found the right man. She told Ma that when the right man came along, she would trade the schoolhouse for her own house gladly.

She missed her family, wrote to them often and planned to spend time with them each summer when school wasn't in session. She had also gone to visit her brother in Amarillo once since she'd come to White Rock.

I could tell by watching that she had plenty of admirers around town. When we had a social and she wore her hair all piled up on her head, she had more cowboys waiting in line for a dance than there were dances. And those cowboys would fight for the pleasure of walking her back to the boardinghouse where she lived.

She was kind to all of them, but Ma said Miss Ross never seemed to encourage any of them because she wasn't particularly interested. She seemed to be content with her life just the way it was—for the present.

She was an interesting lady. She loved to ride out to the canyon where Darby's Creek formed a deep hole. She'd swim for awhile, then read or practice shooting the six-gun or the rifle she carried on those trips. She usually took a picnic lunch, and she sometimes invited Esther or one of the other older girls to go with her. The canyon was pretty much deserted, and she kept her visits to it secret and irregular.

On Sundays, when she sang a solo, her voice was as clear and sweet as it could be. It was soprano, not the deep alto like Ma's voice. When they sang together, Marshal Bodie often said their music must be like angels' music.

In the schoolhouse, Miss Ross was strict, but kind and patient too. She explained things so that all could understand and answered our questions in such a way that we felt glad we had asked them.

Ma invited her to supper on Tuesdays; she accepted and became a part of our evening once a week. I usually waited around after school on

Tuesday until she was ready to go. Then I'd bring her horse to the schoolhouse, or she'd hire a buckboard, and we'd ride to the ranch together.

We'd start the evening with a good meal. After supper, we'd sit and visit, read aloud from a book—something we'd read only on those Tuesday evenings until we had finished it—or sit around our piano and sing all kinds of songs. Ma called those evenings our "family time," and Miss Ross really did get to be like an older sister to me and a younger one to Ma. I only wish that Pa could have been there too.

Well, I reckon I had better get back to my story.

I tied Prince to a rail and walked over to the general store to see Jasper and get something to drink. He had one more year with the younger group in school, so I hadn't had much of a chance to talk to him during the day.

Jasper's hair didn't have that hacked-up look it had had when I first met him. It had been cut close all summer, but now that it was growing out, it looked like a soft, thick bush that stuck out in every direction. Jasper was pretty tall for a ten-year-old, but still the top of his head only came up to my shoulders. He was still a turtle head, but I liked him more than ever.

Jasper had helped at the store all summer, so I hadn't seen much of him during the week, but he had spent Sunday afternoons with me during the summer. He and his family were regular guests at our dinner table after church. They were growing as Christians, and Ma said that hiring Jasper's pa was one of the best decisions she had ever made. The general store had enough business that Ma would have it paid off even earlier than she had expected.

Jasper was behind the counter, grinning as usual, when I walked in. His face lit up even more when he saw me. He was the closest thing to a brother I'd ever had.

"Well, Jasper, how was your first day at school?" I asked. I dug two bits out of my pocket, slapped it on the counter, and ordered each of us a bottle of soda pop. Jasper drank about half of his bottle in one gulp; and then, opening his mouth wide, he let out a roaring belch. Both of us burst out laughing. Then I realized that someone else was in the store.

That someone else was Widow Smith. She and her husband had opened a boardinghouse when the town was just new. One day her husband had just disappeared, and for the last seven or eight years, she'd run the boardinghouse by herself.

Ma and Pa had always taught me that witches were make-believe, but I sometimes wondered when I looked at the widow's face. I reckon she must have been about sixty years old. She was as skinny as a fence rail and straighter than most. Her face was always angry when she marched down the street, looking like she was on her way to tell on someone—and maybe she was. She sometimes spoke to other adults, but never to children unless she was scolding them. She just fixed her eyes on them and shook her head.

She had been walking toward the counter where we stood. When Jasper belched, she had stopped dead still, staring at us. She eyed us both for what must have been half a minute but felt like two days, and I realized that she didn't know which of us had committed the crime.

Suddenly, Jasper whacked me on the back. "Well, Arty, don't just stand there; excuse yourself!"

Before I realized what I was doing, I had said, "Excuse me, ma'am," and Widow Smith had marched past us with a look on her face like she'd been sucking a persimmon. She was mumbling

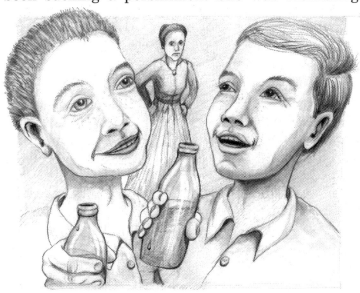

something about children who weren't brought up right as Mr. Wilson was wrapping her goods.

When I looked at Jasper, he was grinning at me. Then I realized what had happened. "Jasper," I whispered, smiling at Widow Smith as she turned her head to glare at us, "I'm going to shake the stuffing out of you as soon as she's gone."

Jasper took another long swig from his pop bottle and grinned at me again. I didn't much like that grin. I'd seen it too many times before, and I knew it meant mischief. Widow Smith had opened the door and turned to give us one more of her hard stares to let us know what she thought of us or put a spell on us—I wasn't sure which. She turned her back and started to close the door.

I was looking at her when I heard a noise like nothing I'd ever heard before. If a pig could talk, his voice would sound like what I heard coming from beside me; but when I looked, only Jasper stood there, eyes wide and mouth gaping. He had let out a long, loud belch, but while it was on the way out, he had said, "Adios!"

As the widow hunched her shoulders and turned, Jasper kept that look on his face and clamped his hand over my mouth. "He's real sorry, ma'am, and didn't mean to be disrespectful or nothing. He just has a sour stomach."

"Sour stomach, indeed!" she said. "Poor upbringing is more likely!"

She was gone before I could pry Jasper's hand

off my mouth. Before I could say anything, the door swung open again, and the widow was looking at Jasper. "Perhaps you should be more careful about the kind of company you keep, young man!" Then she was gone.

Jasper backed up against the wall and slid down until he was sitting on a nail keg. He was laughing hard enough that he was having trouble catching his breath. For a few seconds I wanted to stuff him down into the nail keg, but I controlled myself.

"That was a rotten thing to do, Jasper. What if she goes to my ma? How could you do something like that to me? Why did you do it?"

Jasper was holding his sides and gasping for breath, so he didn't answer. I had one more question for him, and then I couldn't help myself; I broke into a fit of laughter. "Can you teach me to do that?"

We talked for a few more minutes while we finished our soda pop. I bought a peppermint stick for Ma and one for me to eat on the way home, said goodbye to the Wilsons and headed for the corral.

CHAPTER FIVE

Prince was feeling pretty frisky from being cooped up all day, so as soon as we got out of town, I let him run. Prince wasn't a big pony, but he could run like the wind. I just gave a whoop and let him go. When he finally began to tire and slowed to a walk, we were over half a mile from town. I remembered the dead calf and decided to check it out on the way home.

As I rode up to the place where I'd found the calf, Prince began to snort and balk, so I dismounted and left his reins dangling. I knew that he wouldn't go far—like all cow ponies, he'd been trained to stay put as long as his reins were left hanging in front of him.

The body of the calf had been dragged farther up into the rocks, and much of it had been eaten. The ground was too hard for tracks to show, but on a smooth rock I found a single, large, bloody footprint—the track of a big mountain lion. I didn't waste any time getting back to the ranch.

As soon as I could find Bill, I told him about my discovery. He leaned with his elbows resting on the top rail of the corral fence while I talked. When I had finished, he rubbed his chin with a huge gloved hand and thought for a minute before he spoke.

"You say you didn't get a good look at him, Arty? Did you notice his color?"

I had always thought that all mountain lions, or "cougars," as the hands called them, were the same color. Bill set me straight.

"Most of 'em is that same sandy brown, but not Phantom. He's big, black as night, and mean as a snake with his tail on fire. You'd better steer clear of those rocks until Chad, Bo or me can take a look. A couple of our hands thought they might have spotted a big black cat out in that direction, and you ain't ready to tangle with Phantom yet."

"Phantom?" I asked, thinking I must not have heard Bill right.

"He's a black cougar—biggest, meanest and smartest cat I've ever seen or heard of. Most of the ranchers in this part of the country have tried to shoot him, trap him or poison him at some time in the last seven or eight years. He disappears for awhile, and just when folks think he's gone for good, he shows up again."

"How has he gotten clean away from so many people?" I asked.

Bill was still rubbing his whiskered chin. "Oh, he hasn't gotten clean away. I know I've winged him once, and George Simms took off a couple of toes with a bear trap back a year or two ago. We started calling him Phantom because he's black and has been so hard to corner. He seems to be a ghost sometimes."

Bill had been staring off across the corral while he was talking, but he looked at me and spoke as sternly as I ever heard him speak. "Ride wide of any place you think he's been, Arty. I know you're thirteen and nearly a man in some ways. You're a better shot than most men with a pistol and as good as I am with a rifle, but you don't have the savvy yet to go after Phantom. If you see any sign of him again, just tell me or one of the boys—and back off. We've lost more than just a heap of live-stock to that cat."

What Bill was saying hit me like a charging Brahman bull. "You mean Phantom killed a man?" I asked.

Bill's reply was quiet. "Three men and a woman that I know of. Two of the men were cowboys trail-ing him at separate times. The man and woman were homesteaders east of here about thirty miles. They were passing through on their wagon—a husband and wife—and just happened to be sitting at their campfire when Phantom had a fresh wound and was crazy with pain. He didn't eat 'em, but they were all torn up. I don't want that same thing to happen to you, kid, so stay away."

"What if he attacks me?" I was beginning to get my dander up at being treated like a baby. "Should I run away or beg for mercy?"

Bill wasn't smiling when he answered. "You never run from a cougar. Nobody's fast enough—not even if you're on Prince. In a short distance, that cat would have your insides out before you had time to think about what he was doing. I know I might be hurting your pride, pardner, but you're going to have to trust me on this one."

After supper that night, Bill told Ma about the dead calf and mentioned Phantom. As he opened the door to leave, he paused to reassure Ma. "Phantom's luck can't hold forever. One way or another someone will get him." He looked at me and raised his eyebrows. "Remember, that somebody ain't going to be you, pardner."

I waited until I was sure Bill was out of hearing before I turned to Ma. "He's hired help, Ma. I'll not have him telling me what to do!"

"What are you talking about, Artemus?" Ma looked shocked. I realized that I had practically shouted the words at her. Something I didn't understand had been building inside me for some time now—that same old ache in the pit of my stomach, especially at night when I tried to go to sleep or when I was outside practicing with my pistol. Sometimes in a rage I would empty my gun at a jackrabbit, a prairie dog or a sidewinder without even knowing why I was angry. I felt that rage again at being told to avoid Phantom.

"I'm not a baby; I can take care of myself without everybody telling me what to do. Besides, he's not my father. My father's dead—and sometimes I wish I was dead too!"

A shocked look froze on Ma's face until I stopped to catch my breath. Then her face relaxed. I saw tears streaming down her cheeks and realized that I too was crying.

"It ain't right, Ma. He was too good a man to die. Why would a God who says He loves us want to take Pa away from us when we need him so much? Marshal Bodie said in his sermon a few weeks back that everything works together for good to those who love God. How is Pa's dying working to our good?"

Ma got up from her seat and came around the table. She took my arm and led me to what had once been Pa's favorite chair. She cried quietly for a few minutes before she could talk; then she spoke softly.

"I don't know if you'll understand what I'm going to say or not, Artemus, but I'm going to try to talk anyway. I've known for some time now that something was bothering you, and I suspected that this was the problem, but I wanted to wait until you were ready to talk. Are you ready?"

I had a knot in my stomach, and my heart felt like it was full of lead, but I was still too angry to talk about anything, and I told Ma how I felt. I watched as more tears fell from her tightly closed eyes. The house was very quiet, and it was a long time before she spoke.

"My beloved son, you must talk soon. Bitterness or anger toward God just won't do. I won't push the issue, but God won't let you rest until you've cleared things with Him. We'll talk when you're ready."

We stood and faced each other, and she gave me

a hug that forced the breath from me. Then she turned and walked quickly away. After I heard the door to her room close, I turned and headed for my bedroom.

I lay awake crying for a long time that night, being angry with God, choking on the bitterness that I had had tucked away in the back of my heart somewhere.

One morning, a couple of weeks later, I went out to do my chores. I was still angry at most things that moved and a few that didn't.

I shoved Prince away when he nuzzled my pockets, looking for his usual carrot or apple. The knot in my stomach was still there. I ate breakfast with the hands so that I could be gone before Ma got up. The cowboys were too busy planning their day to notice how quiet I was, so I ate and got Grubby to put some lunch in my tin. From the weight of it, I reckoned he'd put enough in it to feed all the boys in my class. He winked at me and grinned.

"Cowboys need to eat to keep up their strength." He squinted at me for a minute. "Arty, you look like you either got a sour stomach or just lost your gal. What's ailing you?"

"Nothing. Thanks for the grub, Grub."

I saddled Prince, stuffed my lunch tin into a saddlebag and put my rifle into its scabbard. The morning sky was cloudless and promised a pretty day—*too pretty a day to sit in school*, I thought. I had been having trouble paying attention lately, even when I was reading "The Legend of Sleepy Hollow" and other stories from *The Sketch Book*, a present from Mr. Travis for helping him butcher a couple of steers.

Since I left the ranch early, I let Prince take his own sweet time about getting to town. My mind began to wander. Pa should be here. He had made a trip out West to see the ranch and buy it. He had probably met Marshal Bodie and some of the ranch hands, but he hadn't gotten to know them. He'd never petted Prince or watched him fly across the open plains at a full gallop with me lying almost flat on his back. He'd never met Miss Ross or Esther or Jasper.

Prince stopped and was looking off to our right at the rocks where I'd found the calf a few weeks before. He snorted and began to prance nervously, like he was standing on Grubby's griddle. His ears were back, and I knew he smelled or heard something that scared him. I patted his neck to calm him.

"Sorry about this morning. I shouldn't be short with you just because I'm out of sorts. You must've gotten a whiff of that old carcass, but I sure would have thought there'd be nothing left to smell by now. Let's go and see."

I could have pointed Prince in any other direction and had him go fine, but he sure didn't want to go toward those rocks. He balked and reared until I finally gave up on him. I forgot—or ignored—everything Luke and the hands had taught me. I ignored the warnings my pony was giving me. I dismounted, pulled my rifle out of the scabbard, and loosened the thong on my six-gun.

"Stay here, you big coward," I whispered. "I'm going to see what's spooking you. It's probably a jackrabbit or a prairie dog."

I worked my way through the scattered sage-brush slowly, watching for any movement in the rocks ahead of me. The sun was almost full up now, and most of the night creatures were gone. I saw a horned toad move a step or two and then stop, hoping I'd go by without seeing him. I crouched, trying to use what little cover there was—moving, then stopping to look and listen the way Bo had taught me: "Don't just use your eyes. Use your ears and your nose too. The good Lord gave them to you for protection, so don't waste them."

I knew that if Prince could smell whatever it was I was hunting, we must be downwind from it so that it couldn't smell me. I still hadn't seen anything when I got to the first of the big rocks that surrounded the foot of the outcrop. I reckon the highest part of that outcrop was only about fifteen or twenty feet high, and the whole thing—not counting the boulders scattered around the base of it—was probably a quarter of a mile long and 150 feet wide.

Still crouching, I worked my way around the point of the outcrop. The breeze brought the faint smell of blood. When I stretched my neck and looked around the edge of the boulder that was hiding me, I saw the back part of a freshly killed steer—probably not a full-grown one from what I could see. Bill had taught me that a kill had to be fresh if the buzzards hadn't found it, and I couldn't see any buzzards from where I was.

I heard a cough, and the hair on the back of my neck stood up. I had never heard the sound before, but I was pretty sure I knew what it was—the cough of a cougar. My hands squeezed my rifle till they hurt, and I started sweating like a convict in a courtroom. My heart was pounding so hard I thought my chest would explode.

I leaned back against a boulder and caught my breath. I needed a clear head if I was going to get this cat. Lying flat on my stomach, I peeked

around a rock and saw the back end of the steer moving with a jerky motion. The cougar was feeding, so he didn't know about me.

I knew I was in a good position to try for a shot. I checked my rifle to be sure there was a cartridge in the chamber. Crawling on my belly, I moved very slowly around the rock. I could see more than half of the steer's body. A huge paw rested on the steer's front quarter, its claws holding the carcass while the awful fangs tore away the meat.

I stopped crawling when I saw the paw. My stomach felt sick, and I wanted to run away. The size of the paw didn't bother me, but the color did. Instead of the tan or gray I had expected, the paw was as black as midnight. It was Phantom's paw.

CHAPTER SIX

I scooted back around the rock like a crawdad running from a coon and sat up with my back against the rock. I felt cold, but sweat was still pouring off me, and I was about as scared as I could be. I just sat there on the ground, trying to calm down enough to think. I knew that Ma, Marshal Bodie, Bill and every cowboy who worked on the ranch would tell me to light a shuck for town or the ranch and get some help. I also knew that if I did go for help, chances were good that Phantom would be long gone before I could get back. I had been told to avoid this black cat, but I had a good chance to kill him right now. After all, he was only a cougar.

Then I made my decision. I was going to take a shot at him. If I missed and he got away, no one else would ever know. If I killed him, how could anyone be angry? Phantom would be dead. I should be able to sneak back around the rock and kill him, hide his body from the buzzards and still get to school on time.

I stretched out on my belly again and crawled back to where I could see the carcass of the steer. With my rifle ready, I slowly scooted forward until I saw the whole steer—or what was left of it. The front part had been chawed some. But the paw I had seen was gone, and when I crawled out a little farther, I saw that the cat had disappeared.

I was so angry I wanted to cry. I had come so

close, and then I had let Phantom get away. Then I thought of something. I knew where Phantom *was not,* but any boy with more brains than a cactus would have been wondering where Phantom *was.* He could have backed away from the steer enough that I couldn't see him. If he had somehow got wind of Prince or me, he might have run off. I hadn't seen him leave, so he had either left the outcrop from the other end, or he was still there, but out of sight.

I was too high-strung to wait for him to show. I had to look for him. Digging my boot toes into the ground, I pulled myself forward with my elbows. Soon I was around the point of the outcrop far enough to see that the dead steer was the only animal there. I don't know how long I had been holding my breath, but I sure felt better after I let it out. I rolled over on my side and let out a sigh. I was disappointed, but at least I could tell Chad I'd seen Phantom. I wouldn't tell him about my trying to kill him though.

A snort, then a squeal from Prince jerked me back to the real world. I had gotten as far as my knees when a scream from the rocks just above me stopped me cold. I kept my body as still as I could while my eyes worked their way up the outcrop. When they reached the top of the point not more than twenty feet above me, I saw Phantom.

His ears were flattened against his head, and his snarl showed a mouthful of huge, yellow fangs. His eyes were green. Now I knew why he had been

named Phantom—he seemed to appear out of nowhere. He looked like what a demon must look like—I was sure. I was also sure he was going to jump on me.

I tried to remember what the hands from the ranch had told me about their experiences with bears, wolves and cougars. Someone had said not to run or make any quick moves. Someone else had talked about staring a wolf down. Bill had said that a cougar could even outrun a pony for a short distance. Bill had also told me to stay away from Phantom.

I was sick with fear, but I knew I had to do something or die. No matter what I did, I would probably die anyway. I kept my eyes on Phantom's eyes. Slowly I began to move my rifle, which was still in my hands but pointing in the opposite direction of the cat.

Phantom snarled and hunched his shoulders. His huge front paws moved closer to the edge of the rock where he sat. He was ready to spring. "God, let me get off one shot before Phantom springs at me," I prayed. My rifle was turned halfway to where it needed to be when he let out a scream and jumped, baring his teeth and claws!

I swung up the rifle, fired it into his body, and rolled over twice to get out of his way. His heavy body hit the barrel of my rifle, ripping it from my hands. I tugged at my six-gun as I rolled over. When I sat up facing the big cat, the hammer was back and the gun was pointed.

Phantom's body was twisted in a strange way, but he was coming at me. I shot him five times at close range—closer than I ever hope to be to a live cougar again. I don't know how many times I thumbed the hammer back and pulled the trigger before I realized my gun was empty, but at the same time, I realized that I was screaming and that Phantom was dead.

I sat on the ground, staring at the cat while I reloaded my pistol with the cartridges from my gun belt. My legs felt weak when I finally stood up. I stepped over the lifeless body, picked up my rifle and checked it to make sure that no sand had gotten inside its works.

Holding it over my head in both hands, I let out a yell: "I got him! I killed Phantom! I killed him by myself!"

I was dancing around the body when I remembered school. I'd have to hustle if I was going to get there on time, but first I had to do something to keep the buzzards away from my prize. They'd surely be after the steer's carcass before I could get back on the way home from school, and then they'd find Phantom's body too.

Suddenly I had an idea. Dragging the dead cougar between two large rocks, I quickly covered his body with smaller rocks and a few bunches of brush. I grabbed my rifle and whistled for Prince. I heard him whinny, but he didn't come the way I had taught him to; he just stood where I'd left him, eyes wide and nostrils flared. I spoke to him softly as I walked toward him; he jumped a little as I reached for his reins. He snorted and reared a little as I mounted, probably because he smelled the scent of the cougar on my hands.

I didn't even have to ask him to hurry. Before I had my second foot in the stirrup, he was heading for town at a dead run.

CHAPTER SEVEN

Miss Ross hadn't started the school day when I walked through the door, but she was standing ready to speak her opening words. I was out of breath, and my shirt was soaked with sweat when I sat down beside Tom Green. He grinned at me and was about to say something when Miss Ross spoke out.

"Good morning, pupils." She looked at me, and I knew she was trying to figure out what I'd been up to. She smiled that pretty smile and asked, "Arty, is Marshal Bodie in town?"

"I think so."

"Then we're probably safe enough that you can hang up your gun." She smiled again and, red-faced, I smiled back.

I was just unbuckling it when I heard Jasper Wilson's cackling voice. "Excuse me, Miss Ross, but, beggin' your pardon, ma'am, I'd like to say that I'd feel a lot safer if I knew I was being protected by an armed man like Artemus Anderson." He grinned at me, closed one eye and pretended to shoot me with his finger. "Then I could put my whole mind to my learning."

"I can lock the door if you get too worried, Jasper," Miss Ross said. "Now let's take some time to read from the Bible."

My shirt had dried some by the time Miss Ross sent us out to eat our lunches. I felt like a cow that hasn't been milked for two days and is about to bust her udder. I had to tell someone what had happened that morning, and the waiting was wearing on me.

We usually ate our lunches out behind the schoolhouse on some old log benches. I reckon they had been made by some former schoolmaster, and years of weather had worn them smooth, although there were plenty of splinters for anyone who tried to slide on them.

Esther, Tom, Jasper and I sat down on the bench that was farthest away from the school-house and the other benches. Tom spoke first.

"Well, come on, Arty! You've never come to school as late as you did this morning, especially not looking like you did. What happened?"

I started to tell my story but stopped when I saw Miss Ross walking toward us. She smiled at us and asked if she could eat with us and listen to my explanation. Tom gave her his place on the bench and sat cross-legged on the ground, facing me.

Now, I really didn't know what to do, and I could tell by their faces that the others didn't either. We ate in silence for what seemed like for-ever; then Miss Ross spoke. "Arty, I'd like to hear too, but I'll leave if I'm preventing you from telling the others."

I nearly choked on a mouthful of food. I couldn't believe how Miss Ross could read what a person was thinking the way she could. I reckoned her hearing my story couldn't hurt anything, so I told it just the way it had happened—more or less.

Miss Ross, Esther and Tom sat with their mouths open, hardly breathing and forgetting about their lunches. Jasper kept eating, but his bulging eyes stared at my face. The further I got in my story, the faster he ate. By the time I had finished, he was stuffing the last of a huge piece of bread into his mouth. With his eyes and cheeks bulged out like that, he looked like some kind of a giant tree toad. He waved his hands and said something that none of us could understand.

I had been watching my listeners while telling the story. Esther was wiping tears from her eyes,

Miss Ross had shuddered a time or two, and Tom's pale face had gotten red because he had been holding his breath. Jasper finished off his mouthful of bread by washing it down with a drink from his canteen. He spoke two syllables, "Un-be—" and the rest came out in a loud hiccup, "lievable!"

Tom fell over on his back, howling with laughter, while Esther and Miss Ross put their hands to their mouths and looked as if they'd just seen a hog slaughtered. Jasper just sat there with his eyes bulging and his turtle head turned a little to one side, waiting to see what would happen. When everything got real quiet, he said in his raspy voice, "Excuse me," and started on another chunk of bread.

Miss Ross and my friends were all excited about my killing Phantom; but they didn't know that I'd been told to ride wide of any sign of him. Esther and Miss Ross told me how brave I was and how proud they were of me. That afternoon Miss Ross asked me to tell the whole school about my adventure. I wasn't sure I wanted to have so many folks know until I'd told Ma, Bill, Chad and the others; but I'd come too far to turn back by then.

Standing in the front of the room, I told my story again in a room so quiet that you could have heard a feather landing on a cotton ball. By the time I finished, I was feeling pretty proud of myself. After all, Phantom was dead, and I wasn't hurt. Things had really panned out pretty well— all things considered.

As soon as Miss Ross turned us loose that afternoon, I lit a shuck for the livery stable. I was saddling Prince when Marshal Bodie came over to the fence. As soon as I saw his face, I knew he'd heard the news. He leaned against a post and chewed thoughtfully on a piece of straw. Neither of us said anything until I was finished and about to lead Prince out of the corral. When he spoke, he spoke softly and calmly, the way I'd known he would.

"Rumor says you got old Phantom this morning. Is that true?"

"Yes sir."

"Interested in the bounty?"

My mouth dropped open, but I managed to close it long enough to ask, "Did you say there was a bounty?"

"When you hand me his ears, I hand you fifty dollars. That's the amount the ranchers collected to give to whoever brought in proof that Phantom was dead. I guess they figured that no one was likely to take off his ears unless he really was dead. Can you get them?"

"Yes sir! I can be back here in less than an hour, and—"

"Hold on there, pardner. Tomorrow morning when you come to school would be soon enough. If the cat you killed is Phantom, there should be a fair-sized chunk gone from one of his ears; he left a piece in one of Henry Lewis's traps last winter. By the way, you'll want to keep the hide from that old devil. I can send a man out to skin him for you if you'll tell me where you left his carcass. We have a couple of good skinners in town who—"

"I can handle things myself!"

The marshal's head jerked around as he looked me in the eye, and I realized I'd almost shouted the words. I was angry, but I had no idea why.

"Son, you've been like a bundle of dynamite with a short fuse for the last few months. What's stuck in your craw? Your Ma is concerned, and I am too. If you want to talk about it, I'll listen."

"I'm sorry, Marshal Bodie; this is something that I have to work out for myself. I'll get someone from the ranch to skin Phantom. He's closer to the ranch than he is to town anyway. Thanks, Marshal. I'm much obliged."

I swung into the saddle, but before I could leave, the marshal had Prince's bridle in his big, brawny hand. Again he spoke softly.

"Arty, your Ma's going to be hurt and probably angry when she gets wind of what has happened. You can't undo what's been done, but I'd advise you to—"

"Thanks, Marshal, but if I can handle Phantom, I can handle my ma. I need to be riding." Without another word, I kicked Prince into a trot and headed for the outcrop where Phantom's carcass was hidden.

I was angry as I let Prince gallop toward the outcrop.

"What I need in my life," I said to Prince, "is another person or two telling me what to do. I'm thirteen years old and almost grown. I'm not a baby, Prince; I'm nearly a man. Pa wouldn't have told me to stay away from Phantom; he'd be proud of me—no, I'll bet he *is* proud of me."

I rode close enough to the outcrop to see that my pile of rocks was just the way I'd left it. Prince was still spooked. I reckon he could still smell the cat. I had my hands full trying to keep him still. I looked at the pale blue sky and spoke again, and I choked back a sob. "O Pa, you are proud of me, aren't you?" I bumped Prince with my heels, and he began to trot toward home.

"O God!" I yelled so loudly that I scared Prince. "Are You happy? You took Pa away from us. Ma says You love us. Marshal Bodie says You work things for our good. How can that be? If things are being worked out for our good, why do I find Ma crying sometimes? Why do I have this ache in my heart and a knot in my stomach? Do You hear me? Do You care? Are You even there, God?"

I drove my fist into the top of my thigh and then wiped my eyes with my sleeve. "Prince, I don't care what any of them has to say. I did what had to be done. They can like it or not!"

CHAPTER EIGHT

I was the last one to the supper table. Bill, Ma and I bowed our heads while Chad gave thanks for the food. Not feeling very hungry, even with a big, juicy steak on my plate, I played with my food and waited for Ma to ask her usual question.

"Well, Arty the Kid, did anything exciting happen today?"

I took a gulp from my coffee cup before I answered her. "On the way to school this morning, I killed Phantom."

Bill and Chad both laughed out loud, and Ma smiled.

"Did you hit him on the head with a rock or wrestle him the way Chad's been learning you?" Bill asked.

"Shucks," said Chad. "I'll bet he throwed his gun on old Phantom and drilled him through the heart before Phantom could even let out a cough."

When they saw that I wasn't laughing, the room got quiet. Ma spoke softly.

"Artemus, please tell me you're teasing us."

Instead, I told them what had happened that morning and mentioned the bounty.

After my story had been told, the four of us just sat there. I looked at them in defiance while they looked at me in amazement.

Bill and Chad started to excuse themselves, but

Ma stopped them. "I'd prefer to have you boys stay, but you may leave if you'd rather."

Both men stayed, and she turned to me. "Not long ago, Bill explained to you that Phantom was a very dangerous animal. He gave you clear directions as to what you were to do if you spotted the animal. From what you've just told us, you simply disregarded his warning and put your life in danger by behaving foolishly." Ma's neck was covered with those red spots, and she had tears in her eyes. "Can you offer any explanation?" she asked.

I couldn't believe the fuss Ma was making over something I reckoned should have made her downright proud of me. I was angry, and I didn't care who knew.

"Ma, I'm thirteen years old. If I'm old enough to carry a gun—which I'm very handy with—then I ought to be able to decide when to use it. As far as what Bill told me, you seem to be forgetting that these cowboys work for us. We don't take orders from hired help. Besides all that, you're kicking a dead horse. You're all riled up about what *could* have happened and not paying any mind to what *did* happen. I *did* kill Phantom, and I *didn't* get a scratch on me. Why can't we just leave it at that?"

The spots were still on Ma's neck, but the tears were gone. What I saw in her eyes and heard in her voice then was anger. She just sat there for a spell, looking at me. When she spoke, it was with authority.

"I am your mother, and I don't expect to hear you use that tone of voice with me again. Maybe what you've proved by this little adventure of yours is that you're *not* ready to carry a gun. As far as taking orders from Bill, Chad, Bo or any of the grown folks on this ranch, you'll do what you're told, or you'll answer to me.

"The fact that you survived without serious injury, or even death, and killed Phantom is more credit to God's mercy and protection than to your ability. I'd like you to wait outside for a few minutes while I talk to Chad and Bill. I'll be out in two or three minutes to tell you what I've decided to do."

Ma was standing now, and I stood to face her. Bill and Chad were still seated and seemed to be studying the floor. I was now taller than Ma, and I looked down at her for a minute. I started to speak but was so angry I choked. I spun on my heel and stomped out of the dining room. Pausing long enough to grab my gun, I strapped it on and stepped out to face the early evening sun.

I was not only angry, I was also hurt. I'd never sassed Ma like this before. I felt sick and wondered if I were just being stubborn. I tried to see Pa and imagine what he would have said. I knew he wouldn't have stood for me being anything but respectful to Ma. "She's the woman of Proverbs 31, Son," he used to say. "Treat her like a precious jewel."

When I heard the door open, I knew I needed to apologize. I turned, and when I saw her face I knew I was in trouble. Chad and Bill had followed her outside, but they were hanging back around the door. She walked to within a few feet of me and stopped, holding out her hand, palm up.

"I'm taking your gun for a month. You're too big for me to whip, but disobedience has to be punished. At the end of a month, we'll see how well I'm pleased with your behavior. Give me your gun, Artemus."

The anger inside me flared, and I forgot about apologizing. "Ma," I said, "you have no right to take my gun. I'm keeping it. Punish me some other way."

"Your gun, Artemus, please."

I took a step back. "I'm not giving up my gun, Ma."

She looked over her shoulder at Bill and Chad, then spoke again. "Gentlemen, could you come here, please."

Both men had been listening. They hesitated, looked at each other, then stepped to Ma's side. These two men had been my friends from the first day we had arrived on the ranch. They had helped teach me to shoot, ride, hunt and do most of the stuff I could do. Chad had been teaching me off and on for almost a year to defend myself, both by wrestling and by using my fists. I owed much to both of them, but I was crazy with anger.

Bill took a step toward me and held out his big, meaty hand. "Son, things will be much better if you'll—"

"Nobody's taking my gun!" I must have shouted because Ma jumped and Bill withdrew his hand. "I'm not your son—I don't have a father. He's dead!" I looked at Ma's face and saw fear. I looked down and realized I was holding my gun. It was pointed at Bill, and it was cocked.

Everything was mighty quiet; then Bill spoke. "Arty, you know better than to draw on a friend. You also know what the Bible says about obeying your parents. Now, I don't understand any better than you do why God took your pa. I don't understand why a lot of things happen, but I know that He loves us and protects us like a special Pa. I know He's never mean and He's never wrong. When I can't understand what He's trying to do, I just have to trust Him. He hasn't let me down yet.

"Your Ma's right, pard. I'm tickled to have Phantom dead; but whether you killed him through luck or through skill, you were dead wrong to disobey your Ma's orders, even though I was the one who gave them. Now, why don't you give her that gun? Then, if it's all right with her, you can take Chad and me to where you buried old Phantom. We'll fetch his carcass back here and skin it for you. Then you can cut off the ears and collect your bounty.

"As for not having your gun for a month, well, I reckon you're just going to have to fess up to having done wrong and then take your punishment like a man."

I lowered my gun and eased back the hammer almost as soon as Bill started talking, and I was crying. I knew without looking that Ma was crying too. I holstered my gun, unbuckled it and stepped toward Ma. She took the gun belt and threw her arms around me, sobbing. I closed my eyes and hugged her, and when I opened them again, Bill and Chad were headed for the barn to get the buckboard.

"O Artemus," Ma whispered, "Bill's right. We can be sad, but we can't be bitter. We can't question God for what He's done. Your father never questioned God's ways in all the years I knew him, and I've tried to follow his example. Isn't there something I can do to help you?"

I waited until I could speak; then I held Ma at arms' length and looked her in the eye. "I'm sorry, Ma. I know I've been wrong in being angry with God. Until today I didn't know how angry I was, but when I drew on Bill—oh, Ma!" I was crying again, and she hugged me for a spell until I could go on. "When I realized that my gun was in my hand—that I might have hurt or even killed Bill because I was angry—I've been so full of anger and hate, I couldn't think straight. Will you forgive me, Ma?" I looked up. "And will You forgive me too, Lord?"

I remembered Pa saying something from time to time about God's children not going by their feelings, but right then I felt something I'll never forget. All of a sudden I felt like someone had lifted a barn off my shoulders. The knot that had been in my stomach for so long was gone, and I felt so good I wanted to laugh out loud or let out a whoop! I wanted to sing. And if I'd been alone, I'd probably have even danced a step or two for joy!

Instead of doing any of those things, I gave Ma a big squeeze and kissed her cheek. She couldn't say anything; she didn't have to.

CHAPTER NINE

Bill and Chad had a team harnessed to the buckboard, and Bo was waiting with them. Chad climbed in back with me; Bill and Bo sat on the seat. Bill clucked to the team, and we were on our way.

Since Bo hadn't been at supper, I had to tell my story again. I included the part about Ma taking away my gun for a month. I asked Bill and Chad to forgive me for my foolishness. They both looked over their shoulders at me, and Bill said, "Son, if you was my own boy, I couldn't be prouder of you than I am for the way you straightened things out with your ma tonight. I'll grant that what you done was wrong, and I reckon your ma's punishment was fair. You just make dead sure you don't let something like this happen again. Chad and me forgive you, and we'll forget the whole thing ever happened, just like we did with Bo."

"Hey," yelled Bo, "you gave me your word you'd never tell anyone about that!"

"About what?" asked Chad. "Bill, what's this boy talking about?"

Bill swung his arm up on the back of the seat and grinned. He winked at me and said, "We wasn't telling anything to anybody, Bo. If anybody tells your tale, it'll have to be you."

"What happened, Bo?" I asked.

Bo leaned back against the side of the buckboard and stretched out his long legs. Folding his big, rough hands on his lap, he just sat looking at them for a minute or two. Reaching up with his left hand, he tipped his hat back, ran his open hand from his forehead to his chin, let out a big sigh, then spoke.

"Arty, I'm considerable younger than these two hombres; and when I came out here six or seven years ago, I wasn't a whole lot older than you are. I had some money; I was cocky and wild." Bo stopped and looked me in the face. "You understand this is just for us to know—you won't tell anyone else, will you?"

"I promise," I quickly answered.

"Well, one day a couple of polecats drygulched me three or four miles outside of town. They got the drop on me after riding up real friendly. They knocked me out, and when I came to, all my money was gone. I was a little green in those days."

"Yeah," said Bill, "we've really improved him a lot since then!"

"Very funny!" said Bo. "Anyway, I couldn't follow a trail and didn't think to look for one anyway. I just rode hard, trying to catch up with the two men and hoping I'd guessed the right direction. When I caught sight of two riders, I started shooting as soon as I was within range. Lucky for me, I was too angry to shoot straight."

"Lucky for us, you mean!" Chad said.

"You mean you were shooting at Bill and Chad?" I asked.

Bo looked at his hands again. "Yes, I thought I had the same men. Anybody else would have killed me, but when they realized I was out of bullets, Bill charged right at me while I was trying to reload. He dropped his lariat over me, and I was on the ground and hog-tied in no time. I was screaming and swearing and threatening these two, and they started laughing. The more they laughed, the more I threatened to kill both of them. Finally, after they'd had a good laugh, Bill took my six-shooter and rifle away from me. Then he untied me and told me that 'little boys' had no business playing with guns. He gave me his name and directions to the ranch and told me that when I grew up I'd know where I could pick up my guns."

"It was two weeks before he could swallow his pride enough to show his face at the ranch," Chad said.

"When I showed up, I had no money and was hungrier than I'd ever been in my life. Bill was foreman for the other owner then. He gave me a meal and a job, but I had to wait another week before I got my guns back."

"We had to make sure he wasn't going to start shooting at us again," said Bill. "Of course, by the time he'd swallowed his pride enough to apologize to us two or three times, we'd decided there might be some good in this sorry varmint, so we kept him around.

"As long as he doesn't start shooting at us again, we'll let him stay."

We all laughed—even Bo—but his face was a little red. We were almost at the outcrop, so I showed Bill where the grave was. Ten minutes later we had the cougar's stiff body uncovered and lying in the back of the buckboard. Bill examined the carcass while the rest of us stood around watching, not saying a word. I don't think I was even breathing.

Bill looked at me and grinned. "Well, I reckon two things are sure. That's dead sure Phantom, and Phantom is sure dead. He's been shot six times, and one of the bullets must've gone through his heart. Let's get this old carcass home and skin it for Arty the Kid. What do you say to that, Kid?"

I didn't say anything. I just hopped onto the buckboard, and we headed for home. All the way back to the ranch and while we were skinning Phantom and scraping his hide to make it fit to use, we laughed and talked. Some of the hands stopped by to see if Phantom were really dead and to congratulate me or tease me about having killed him.

Then the stories started. We heard tales about cowboys who had fought cougars, bears or wolves when there was no ammunition left or when the cowboys had been wounded or when the animals had outnumbered the humans ten to one. Each cowboy told his story as poker-faced as he could, but the rest of the bunch chuckled, imitated the

calls of the animals being described or just laughed right out loud.

After things had settled down a bit, Grubby came over to the group that was left, cut off a chaw of tobacco and sat down on an old stump we used for a chopping block. He chewed for a while, then tucked his quid into one cheek and started to talk in that old Texas drawl of his.

"You boys have been telling some pretty fair tales, and I don't mean to put you down, but by the time you was big enough to tote a gun, some of us older gents had pretty much whipped the tar out of the wildest things in the country. You know, we'd killed most of the buffalo, the fiercest Injuns, the biggest bear and wolf and cougar. Why, cats like Phantom we kept for *pets*."

The sun was sinking, but there was still plenty of light to show Grub's expression. He chewed a time or two on his quid, then tucked it away again before he continued.

"I recollect one time I was coming back from somewhere when I got caught in a blizzard. Snow was falling, and the wind was blowing so hard I couldn't tell where I was. After wandering for a day or two without stopping to eat or sleep, I finally had to make camp because my horse was tired. The snow was about six feet deep and hard to get through, but we finally found a cave in the side of a hill."

"How'd you find the cave in six feet of snow?" Bill asked.

Grubby chewed for a minute and rubbed one hand over his bristling chin whiskers. "Well now, finding that cave was about the best piece of luck I ever had, and I figure it came my way on account of my riding my lucky horse. I had a little black mare I named Lucky because whenever I rode her anywhere, good things just seemed to happen to me."

"Good things like getting stuck in a blizzard?" asked one of the cowboys.

Grubby chewed his quid until the laughter quieted down. "Getting stranded in a blizzard wasn't good luck, but finding the cave was, at least for me. You see, the cave weren't a very big one, so there was room only for me and that grizzly bear in there—"

"Wait just a minute, Grub! You never mentioned a grizzly bear."

"That's because I just now got to that part of the story. Hold your horses! Now, as I was saying, the cave was on the small side, so I had to leave Lucky out in the snow. When I got into that cave, there was the biggest grizzly I'd ever seen, snoring away. Even though I was out of the snow, I knew I'd soon be frozen if I couldn't find a way to keep warm. I'd lost my flint two days before, so I had no way to build a fire. I knew there was only one thing to do."

"What did you do?" I asked. I looked around and noticed the hands were grinning as much at me as they were at Grub. I was really caught up in his story, but I noticed that some of them were too.

"Well now, I was out of ammunition too, so I took out my knife, slit open that grizzly's belly and crawled inside to keep warm."

"I've heard of other hombres who've done the same thing," said Bo. "What's so special about—"

"I'm getting there; stop interrupting me." Grubby spat in the dust, then continued. "Well, I curled up inside that old Grizzly and went to sleep. When I woke up, I couldn't recollect where I was. It was warm all right, but it was pitch dark, and the smell was terrible. Then I realized what had happened. While I'd been asleep, the slit I'd made in that old grizzly had healed shut, and I was stuck inside him.

"I wasn't too worried because my twelve-inch, razor-sharp bowie knife, a pearl-handled beauty with a diamond set in each side of the handle, would get me out as easily as I got in. I felt for it, but it was gone. I was trapped."

Grubby spit again, wiped the back of his hand across his mouth and went on with his story.

"Well, I didn't want to wind up being digested by that grizzly, so I decided if one of us had to be et by the other, I'd rather be the one doing the eating. I had most of my teeth back then, so I just found a likely spot and started chawing. That bear was all stored up with fat for the winter, so chawing my way out took time. By the time I got through—I was only eating two meals a day on account of having no coffee to go with them—that grizzly was just a dead, empty skin. Spring had come, and I weighed near a hundred pounds more than I'd ever weighed before. I came out of that cave to find no sign of Lucky. My saddle and bridle were on the ground, so I figured she'd froze and then the wolves had et her.

"I wanted to bring that grizzly's hide with me when I came back to where there was people, but I had to walk near fifty miles to get to a trapper's cabin. By then I didn't have an urge to go back to the cave just for the hide. If the wolves hadn't chewed the saddle so, I would have carried it out with me. It was black with silver studs, and so was the bridle."

"Now, you're telling us that this story is true, Grub?" Chad asked.

Grub sat up straight, shifted his quid to his left cheek and looked around. "Any of you boys ever see me on a black mare named Lucky?"

We all shook our heads.

"Anybody ever see me with a black, silver-studded saddle or bridle?"

We shook our heads again.

"Has anyone ever seen me with a pearl-handled, twelve-inch, diamond-studded pig sticker?"

Behind me a couple of voices said, "No!"

The old man turned slowly and began his bow-legged walk toward the bunkhouse. After ten or twelve paces, he turned to face us. "Then how," he asked in his crackly voice, "can you doubt my story? Come with me, Arty."

With that he turned and marched into the bunkhouse, leaving the door open behind him. "Close the door, son, and sit down," he said as I walked into the bunkhouse. I sat on his bed beside him. For a long time he said nothing. When he turned his head and looked at me, I saw sadness in his eyes.

"Sometimes I'm a loose-tongued old fool. I've never told anyone else the things I told you a few days ago. I guess I told you because you're easy to talk to. I saw that I'd hurt you, and then I watched what happened between you and Bill. I know that what happened is at least partly my fault, and I'm sorry. Talking to you like I did the other day was like letting the infection out of a wound. I feel different—like maybe there's still some hope somewhere. I guess I'm asking you to forgive me and to...well...say a prayer for me now and again, when you think of it."

"I will, Grubby!" I threw my arms around his neck and gave him a hug, feeling sure it was the first one he'd had in a long, long time. After saying goodnight, I walked back to where the hands were, hoping to hear one more good story before I went to bed.

CHAPTER TEN

After listening to two more stories, I said good-night and walked back to the house. Ma was sitting in the parlor. She closed her book and smiled at me. I sat down on the floor beside her chair, and she laid her hand on my shoulder. "Hello, handsome," she said. "Are you still my friend?" I told her that I loved her, and I turned my head, but not before she saw the tears in my eyes.

"Arty, something is still not right. Please talk to me. Even if I can't help, sometimes just telling someone else your troubles makes you feel better." I thought of what Grubby had told me, and I knew

that there was no one else I could talk to the way I could talk to her.

"Ma," I said, "I don't think I'm bitter about Pa's dying. At least I try not to be." I had to stop for a minute. I couldn't look at Ma, but I knew she was crying too. "I just don't understand what good came of it. I'm sure Pa's happy, but I miss him. And what about you? You're still young and beautiful, and you have to be by yourself."

"I have you, Artemus, and some good friends," Ma said.

"I mean you don't have a husband. I know you're lonely. It's been almost three years now. I started a year ago asking God to give you another husband. I wouldn't mind, and I don't think Pa would. I've been praying that we wouldn't hurt so bad too, but God hasn't answered my prayer. If He's not going to answer the most important prayers I have, why should I bother praying about anything else? Sometimes I don't think God cares."

Ma was quiet for a minute. "Artemus, I don't understand why God took your father away from us either, but I do know that He loves us more than even your father did and that He only does what's best for us. I know that as much as it hurts me when I see you hurt, it hurts God more. I know that someday, maybe not before we get to Heaven, we'll understand. In the meantime, we have to believe what God tells us, trust Him and go on with our lives."

"Should we just grit our teeth and try to make the best of life?" I asked.

"Oh no, Artemus, no!" Ma replied. "As Christians, we should be full of joy and hope because of what we have in Christ. We're rich in blessings! We need to focus on what God has given us, not what He has taken away."

It was a long time before I went to sleep that night. Before I did, though, I promised God that I'd try to trust Him the way Ma did and to enjoy what He had given me. I knew that Ma was right. We had a lot we could be happy about.

Ma had to call me twice to get me out of bed the next morning. Usually I was up before she was, but I was tired. I ate breakfast with her and told her about what I had decided. She smiled. "We can do what we need to with God's help."

I felt mighty strange riding unarmed to school that morning. I had been hoping that I could get to school early enough that I could be inside the schoolhouse before the other students showed up, but I had to gallop Prince part of the way just to make sure I got there on time. I was still hoping that no one would notice as I walked in and sat down.

Miss Ross was still sitting at her desk, but she was about to begin when Esther's little sister, Ruth, said, "Arty, you forgot your gun!"

Everybody's eyes, even Miss Ross's, were turned toward me. I felt hot, and I knew my face was red, but I just sat down quietly beside Tom Green. Miss Ross stood up to start school, and I was safe until lunchtime.

All morning I had trouble keeping my mind on my studies. I was trying to think of something I could tell my friends that would keep them from recognizing me as the fool I had been. When Miss Ross dismissed us for lunch, I knew I had to tell them the truth.

When I finished my story, they were all quiet except for Jasper. He was sitting on the ground, licking some cherry pie from his fingers. Miss Ross spoke first.

"Your mother did the right thing, Arty. What you did was wrong, and you had to be punished, but your reaction to that punishment shows me that you're growing into a young man who's going to make your family and friends proud of you. I know I am."

Esther was sitting beside me. "I'm proud of you too, Arty, for accepting your punishment with the right spirit and for admitting to us that you were wrong." She smiled at me in a way that made me want to tell the whole story again.

Tom grinned at me and slapped me on the back. "I'm glad you're my pardner, Arty."

Miss Ross got up from the bench. "We need to get back to work soon, Artemus; you had better eat your lunch."

Esther and Tom walked toward the schoolhouse, and Jasper came over to sit beside me. He was quiet for a minute. "I'm proud of you too, Arty. I want to be like you when I grow up." He stood, took three or four steps toward the schoolhouse, then stopped. His turtle head turned to look over his shoulder at me, and he grinned. "Are you going to finish your cake?"

I couldn't help grinning at him. "What's the magic word, you little buzzard?" I asked.

Jasper's face lit up, and with a gushing sound that was more like a roar, he said, "Please!"

CHAPTER ELEVEN

That month without my gun seemed like a year, but I reckon I did some growing up during that time. Two or three times each week, I rode out to Coyote Canyon, where I had learned to shoot. I took my Bible and something to eat and spent time trying to sort out some things in my mind. I had been wrong to be angry with God for letting Pa die, but I still hurt even after these three years, and I didn't know what to do to stop the pain.

One day after school, I left Prince to nibble at a small patch of grass at the canyon's mouth. I climbed up to the top of a huge boulder that was shaped just right for me to sit with my back propped against the highest part of it and stretch out my legs in front of me. Sitting there in the sun, I dozed off for a few minutes. The sound of Prince's whinny woke me, and I instinctively reached for my six-gun. Then I remembered that Ma had it.

When I stood up, I could see Ma and Marshal Bodie dismounting near where I'd left Prince. They spotted me when I waved and then headed in my direction. I slid to the ground and stood waiting for them. Ma had never been to the canyon before, but her smiling face convinced me that no trouble brought her here on her first visit.

"Luke said we'd probably find you here," she said. "It's beautiful, Artemus. I can understand why you come here."

"I can understand why I come here too," I said, "but I don't understand why you're here."

Marshal Bodie took off his hat, ran his fingers through his hair, then put it on again. "What have you been doing, Arty?" he asked.

I was pretty sure both of them knew, but I answered him anyway. "Thinking and praying, I reckon."

"Did we interrupt?" asked Ma.

"Shucks, no, Ma. I was doing more napping than anything else. Besides, no man worth his salt would consider his ma an interruption anyway." I took her hand in mine and squeezed it.

We walked up the canyon a ways. Ma stopped and pointed at a greasewood bush with some tins hanging on it. "That's what I came to see," she said. "For all the bragging I've heard about your shooting, I thought those tins would have more holes in them than they do. You haven't been stretching the truth, have you?"

Before I could answer, Marshal Bodie spoke. "Ma'am, you'd best mind what you say. That hombre is Arty the Kid, and he don't take to being called a liar."

Ma's eyes opened wide. She put one hand to her mouth and the other on the marshal's arm. Then she threw her head back and laughed. "Arty the Kid? Why, this hombre isn't even wearing a gun. You must be mistaken, sir."

The marshal looked at me through squinting

eyes. "Oh, that's the Kid, ma'am. I know; I've seen him shoot. Why, right over there at that bush he took on the Tin Can Gang and shot four of them single-handedly in one day. He's lightning, ma'am—pure lightning."

Ma stuck her nose in the air and looked at me from the corner of her eye. "Well, sir, I'm afraid I'd have to see with my own eyes before I could believe it! Oh, look!" She pointed at the bush. "The rest of the Tin Can Gang has come to town. Save me, Marshal! Save me!"

Marshal Bodie stepped behind Ma and tried to hide. "There are six this time, ma'am—too many for me."

"What will we do?" asked Ma.

"The Kid stopped them once; he'll have to do it again," said the marshal.

"But he's unarmed!" Ma said.

Marshal Bodie winked at me, grinned just a bit, and tossed me some saddlebags that he had slung over his shoulder. "Not anymore," he said. "His parole ended yesterday, and he gets his gun back."

Suddenly I understood what they were up to. Inside one of the saddlebags, I found my six-gun in its holster. Loading it quickly, I buckled on the belt, tied down the holster, pushed my hat back on my head and looked at Ma.

"You and your pal stand aside, ma'am. I'll take care of the Tin Can Gang once and for all." I turned and took half a dozen steps toward the tin bush.

"Make your play," I said. There were six tins on the bush. I drew and fired five quick shots, and with each shot a tin jumped from the bush. I spun my gun into its holster so smoothly I almost laughed from surprise.

"You're safe now, ma'am," I said, walking back toward Ma and the marshal.

Ma looked a little stunned, but she said, "Kid, what about the one you left alive?"

I looked as offended as I could and said, "Arty the Kid never shoots women, ma'am!"

As we walked back to the horses, we were laughing so hard that I had trouble reloading my gun. Riding home, I realized that my heart felt light. I didn't have all of the answers I was looking for, but I knew that somehow God was going to work things out for the best. I made up my mind right there that I was going to trust Him to do whatever needed to be done and do it His way.